For my grandchildren,
who are learning to keep
their elbows off the table
—H.M.Z.

For my Mom,
who taught me that it doesn't matter
which spoon you start with,
so long as you don't slurp
—P.C.

Text copyright © 2008 by Harriet Ziefert
Illustrations copyright © 2008 by Pascale Constantin
Book design by Elliot Kreloff
All rights reserved
CIP Data is available.
🍎 Blue Apple Books
515 Valley Street, Maplewood, NJ 07040
www.blueapplebooks.com
Distributed in the U.S. by Chronicle Books
First Edition
Printed in China

ISBN: 978-1-934706-02-2

1 3 5 7 9 10 8 6 4 2

Mother Goose

Manners

Harriet Ziefert

Illustrations by
Pascale Constantin

BLUE APPLE BOOKS

Little Jack Horner
Sat in a corner,
Eating a Christmas pie.
He put in his thumb
And pulled out a plum
And said,
"What a good boy am I."

What *should* Jack have said?

Little Miss Tuckett
Sat on a bucket,
Eating some peaches and cream.
There came a grasshopper
And tried hard to stop her,
But she said,
"Go away, or I'll scream."

What *should* Jack have said?

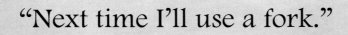

"Next time I'll use a fork."

Little Miss Tuckett

Sat on a bucket,

Eating some peaches and cream.

There came a grasshopper

And tried hard to stop her,

But she said,

"Go away, or I'll scream."

What *should* Miss Tuckett have said?

"Grasshopper,
would you like a taste?"

Nobody loves me,

Everybody hates me,

I'm going out to eat worms.

Long, skinny, slimy ones,

Big, fat, juicy ones,

Itsy bitsy, teeny ones.

See how they wiggle and squirm.

Yum! Yum!

What *should* you do after eating?

Wipe your mouth with a napkin,
and wash your hands and face.

There once was a fish.

(What more could you wish?)

He lived in the sea.

(Where else would he be?)

He was caught on a line.

(Whose line if not mine?)

So I brought him to you.

(What else should I do?)

What do you say?

"Thank you very much
for the gift."

Oh, the cow kicked Nelly

In the belly in the barn,

The cow kicked Nelly

In the belly in the barn,

The cow kicked Nelly

In the belly in the barn,

But the farmer said it

Would do no harm.

What *should* the cow have said?

"Sorry, Nelly. I didn't mean to hurt you."

Pussycat, pussycat,
Where have you been?
I've been to London
To visit the queen.

Pussycat, pussycat,
What did you there?
I frightened
A little mouse
under
Her chair.

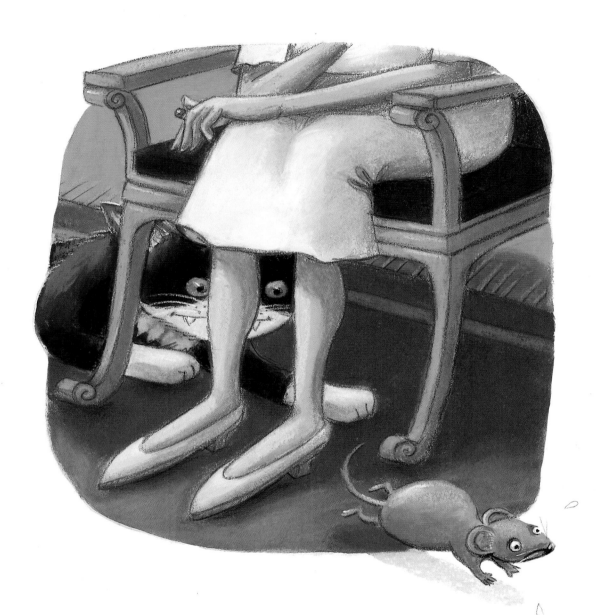

What *should* the pussycat have said?

"Excuse me, mouse.
Don't be scared.
I won't hurt you."

There was an old woman
Called Nothing~at~all,
Who lived in a dwelling
Exceedingly small.
A man stretched his mouth
To its utmost extent,
And down at one gulp
House and old woman went.

What *should* the man have done?

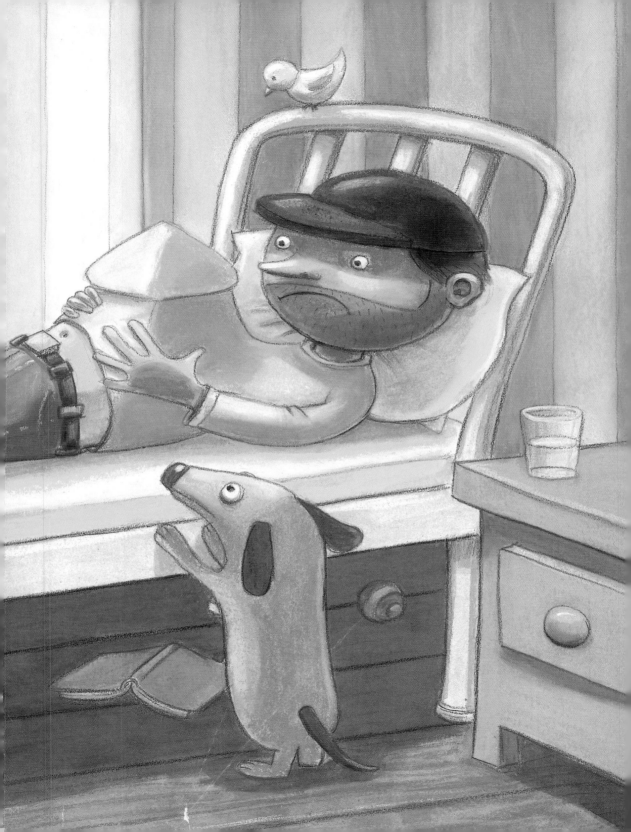

He should have chewed his food
before swallowing.

Jack Sprat
Could eat no fat,
His wife
Could eat no lean,
And so between them both,
You see,
They licked the
platter
clean.

What *should* the Sprats have done?

They should have used
knives and forks.

Three little kittens,
They lost their mittens,
And they began to cry,
"Oh, Mother dear, we sadly fear
That we have lost our mittens."
"What! Lost your mittens,
You naughty kittens!
Then you shall have no pie."

The three little kittens,
They found their mittens,
And they began to cry,
"Oh, Mother dear, see here, see here,
Our mittens we have found."
"Put on your mittens, you silly kittens,
And you shall have some pie."

The three little kittens
Put on their mittens
And soon ate up the pie.
"Oh, Mother dear, we greatly fear
That we have soiled our mittens."
"What! Soiled your mittens,
You naughty kittens!"
Then they began to sigh,
Mee-ow, mee-ow, mee-ow,
Then they began to sigh.

What *should* the kittens have done?

They should have removed
their mittens before eating.

Little Miss Muffet sat on a tuffet
Eating her curds and whey.
Along came a spider
And sat down beside her
And frightened
Miss Muffet away.

What *should* the spider have asked?

"Excuse me, is this seat taken?"

This little pig
Went to market,
 This little pig
Stayed home.

This little pig
Had roast beef,
 This little pig
Had none.

And this little pig cried
"Wee-wee-wee"
All the way home.

What *should* the wee pig have done?

Instead of whining, he should have offered to help carry the packages.

Davy, Davy Dumpling
Boil him in a pot,
Sugar him
And butter him,
And eat him while he's hot.

Wait till everyone is served
before you start.